BRIAN GALLAGHER was born in Dublin. He is a full-time writer whose plays and short stories have been produced in Ireland, Britain and Canada. He has worked extensively in radio and television, writing many dramas and documentaries.

Brian is the author of four adult novels, and his other books of historical fiction for young readers are *Friend or Foe* – the prequel to *One Good Turn* – *Across the Divide*, set during the 1913 Lockout; *Taking Sides*, which takes place against the backdrop of the Civil War; *Secrets and Shadows*, a spy novel that begins with the North Strand bombings during the Second World War; and *Stormclouds*, set in Northern Ireland during the turbulent summer of 1969. His next book, *Arrivals*, is set in Canada in the summer of 1928. Brian lives with his family in Dublin.

ONE GOOD TURN

1916

HOW MUCH DO YOU RISK TO PAY BACK A FAVOUR?

BRIAN GALLAGHER

THE O'BRIEN PRESS
DUBLIN

First published 2016 by The O'Brien Press Ltd.,
12 Terenure Road East, Rathgar, Dublin 6, D06 HD27, Ireland.
Tel: +353 1 4923333; Fax: +353 1 4922777
E-mail: books@obrien.ie
Website: www.obrien.ie
The O'Brien Press is a member of Publishing Ireland.

ISBN: 978-1-84717-817-6

10 9 8 7 6 5 4 3 2 1
20 19 18 17 16

Layout and design: The O'Brien Press Ltd.
Printed and bound by CPI Group (UK) Ltd, Croydon, CR0 4YY

The paper in this book is produced using pulp from
managed forests.

DEDICATION

In memory of Kathleen Kelly

ACKNOWLEDGMENTS

My sincere thanks to The O'Brien Press for inviting me to write a novel for World Book Day, and to my editor, Nicola Reddy, for her skilful editing and advice, and for suggesting Gerry Quinn – a minor character in my book *Friend or Foe* – as a possible central character in *One Good Turn*.

To publicists Ruth Heneghan, Geraldine Feehily and Carol Hurley for all their efforts on my behalf, to Emma Byrne for her usual excellent work on cover design, and to everyone else at The O'Brien Press, with whom, as ever, it's a pleasure to work.

My thanks also go to Hugh McCusker for his painstaking proofreading,

And finally, no amount of thanks could express my gratitude for the constant support and encouragement of my family, Miriam, Orla and Peter.

PROLOGUE

EASTER TUESDAY, APRIL 25TH, 1916
Talbot Street, Dublin

GERRY QUINN WATCHED as the looters smashed shop windows, his heart pounding with excitement. It was only a day since the first shots had been fired in the Rising, and he was surprised that law and order had broken down so quickly. He felt a guilty thrill now as he saw a red-faced man swinging a pickaxe at the window of a men's clothes shop. The glass in the window shattered, and the man entered the shop, followed by cheering looters.

Gerry was tempted to follow, though he knew that if he was caught he would be in huge trouble. He couldn't be put in jail, because he was only thirteen, but the reformatories where he could be sent had fearsome reputations. Not to mention the beating his Uncle Pat would give him if he was arrested.

Since the death of his parents in an accident when he was six, Gerry had lived with his uncle in a ramshackle cottage by the River Tolka. Even when Uncle Pat wasn't drunk, it was a tough life. Gerry had to work each day after school on Pat's cart, collecting slops for piggeries. But his uncle was sleeping off a feed of whiskey from last night and had no idea that Gerry had slipped into town.

Besides, the chances of being arrested were slim – the unarmed Dublin Metropolitan Police had been withdrawn to barracks after two of their members were shot dead yesterday.

Rumour had it that thousands of soldiers were on their way from Britain to fight the rebels of the Irish Volunteers and the Citizen Army, so Gerry knew he had to act fast. Even so, he hesitated outside the shop. He had heard that the rebels were against looting, and that they were firing shots towards looters to discourage them. But there were poor people in Dublin for whom this was the chance of a lifetime, and nothing would stop them from helping themselves.

Although Gerry had been poor all his life, he had never been a thief. Every winter, though, he shivered in Uncle Pat's freezing cottage and out on their cart – and now there was a chance to end that, with a store full of fine clothes at his disposal. He stood, uncertain, on the sunlit pavement, then two women in black shawls went around him and into the shop. Gerry realised that if he didn't act soon, the place would be cleared out. Without agonising any more, he followed the shawled women.

He stepped gingerly over jagged glass as he climbed in the front window. The mannequins that had stood in the window were already being stripped, and Gerry moved on into the cool interior of the shop.

People were grabbing everything in sight. A couple of men tussled over a tweed suit, while another man donned a bowler hat, laughing. Gerry could see that a carnival atmosphere had developed among the looters.

'Are you looking for boyswear, son?!' asked one of the shawled women playfully.

The other shawled woman spoke to Gerry in a put-on posh voice. 'We've some lovely new stock, if Sir would like to try it!'

Gerry grinned, and the woman reverted to her Dublin accent. 'They've stuff for young fellas at the back, son, but it's going fast.'

'Thanks, missus,' he said, then he moved past her as other looters exited the shop, their arms full of clothes.

Gerry decided that above all he needed an overcoat for next winter, and he ignored the summer shirts and trousers. Much of the clothing was now on the floor, but he stepped over the mess and finally found a rail of overcoats. He was undergoing a growth spurt this year, so he picked a Crombie that was slightly large for him. He admired the rich texture of the coat's material, then grabbed a couple of pullovers and two boxed shirts and, his arms full, turned and made for the front of the shop.

'Well may ye wear, son!' cried one of the shawled women, as she and her friend filled two large sacks with clothes.

'Thanks,' said Gerry, then he retraced his steps over the broken glass and out the shop window onto Talbot Street.

He could hear machine-gun fire in the distance, and the air was heavy with smoke from a burning building. His heart was thumping. Gerry knew that he looked like a looter now; shots could be fired in his direction by the rebels at North Earl Street. Eager to get away from the danger zone, he ran towards Marlborough Street, colliding with a bicycle as he rounded the corner.

'Watch where you're going!' cried the cyclist, a red-haired man in his mid-twenties who barely managed to stay upright after braking suddenly.

'Sorry, mister!'

The man looked really angry and he glowered at Gerry, who was quickly gathering the looted clothes. 'Sorry mister, but no harm done!'

Before the man could respond, Gerry set off again at speed, heading up by the Pro Cathedral. The morning was hot, and Gerry began to sweat as he ran through the war-torn city. He knew that he couldn't run all the way home, burdened as he was, so he slowed down.

Now that his initial excitement had lessened, it was time to think clearly. Maybe he shouldn't run at all – it only drew attention. Then again, even if he folded the clothes neatly, anyone he met would still guess that he was a looter. *Well, let them!* This had been a unique opportunity, and Gerry wasn't ashamed that he had taken it. In fact, if there were any grocery shops being looted between here and home, he'd try to get some food as well – he was tired of bad meals and having to go without.

He walked on briskly and was approaching the corner of Gloucester Street when a voice rang out: 'Halt there!'

Gerry was startled, and he cursed himself for dreaming about food instead of concentrating on his escape. One wrong move here could get him shot. He forced himself to turn around very slowly, holding his breath.

A man in an Irish Volunteers uniform was approaching, with a Mauser rifle aimed at Gerry's chest. 'What do you think you're doing?' he said.

Gerry thought it was obvious what he was doing, so he said nothing.

'Dirty little looter!' said the man, in what Gerry recognised as a middle-class accent. Now that the Volunteer had drawn near, Gerry could see that he was young, perhaps only nineteen or twenty.

'We're risking our lives for Ireland,' the Volunteer continued, 'and all you slum rats do is help yourselves!'

Despite his predicament, Gerry felt a surge of anger. 'Who asked you to risk your life for Ireland?!'

The man looked taken aback, so Gerry kept going. 'You've never been hungry, have you? Or freezing with the cold?' He indicated the heavy overcoat that he had stolen. 'Well, next winter I won't be either! And if you don't like that, you can lump it!'

'Don't cheek me, you pup! You can turn right around and bring those clothes back where you got them.'

Gerry's pulses were racing. Being called a slum rat had really annoyed him. He looked the man squarely in the eye. 'No,' he said firmly.

'What?'

'It makes no sense. Someone else would just take them.'

The Volunteer raised the stock of the rifle to his shoulder and took careful aim. 'Looters can be shot. Your choice. Bring the stuff back, or else.'

Gerry felt his stomach tighten. It wasn't worth dying for an overcoat, he told himself. But would the Volunteer really shoot him? Gerry had been in lots of fights, and he could usually tell if an opponent was tough. And despite the Volunteer's fighting talk, Gerry sensed that he wouldn't be ruthless enough to shoot a thirteen-year-old boy.

'No, it's *your* choice,' said Gerry. 'You can fight the British, like you're supposed to be doing, or you can shoot a kid.'

The man looked uncomfortable, and Gerry decided to go for broke. 'I'm going home now. You can shoot me in the back, or you can go back to fighting your real enemy. Good luck if you decide to fight.' He started to move off.

'Stop or I'll shoot!' shouted the Volunteer.

Gerry felt his mouth go dry, and he hoped that he hadn't miscalculated.

'I mean it!' cried the rebel.

Gerry had only a split second to decide: stop and lose all of the clothes, or go with his instincts and risk a bullet. Time seemed to freeze, and he held his breath but kept walking. Gloucester Street was up ahead, and once around the corner he would be out of sight of the Volunteer. He kept going, dreading the impact of a bullet in his back.

The Volunteers had been drilling for years, but this was their first real battle. Gerry told himself that the young man was just playing at being a soldier and wouldn't have the stomach to shoot a boy. But on the other hand, maybe he was impulsive, and his pride mightn't let him be bested by a thirteen-year-old.

'I won't tell you again!' cried the man.

Gerry thought the warning sounded more desperate than threatening, and he forced himself to keep going. The corner was drawing near, and if the Volunteer was going to shoot, it had to be in the next second or two. Gerry bit his lip, knowing this was foolish yet determined to get the better of the man.

He took a deep breath as he came to Gloucester Street. It would be unbearable to come this far only to be shot at the last moment. He felt his muscles tensing, but a few steps later he knew he was safe. He breathed out a huge sigh of relief, turned the corner and made for home.

CHAPTER ONE

FRIDAY,
AUGUST 4TH, 1916

EMER HATED SERVING Mrs Andrews, and she sighed inwardly as the woman stepped into Davey's grocery shop wearing her usual severe grey suit.

Mrs Andrews was gaunt and rarely smiled, and Emer thought that this morning she looked even more poker-faced than usual. But Mrs Andrews ran a large bed and breakfast nearby, which made her a valued customer. And Dad had two golden rules: make every customer welcome, and the customer is always right.

'Good morning, Mrs Andrews,' said Emer pleasantly. 'Lovely weather.'

'Oppressively hot.'

What a moaner! thought Emer. Her father had a knack of getting on with all his customers, even the grumpy ones, and Emer wished that he was here right now. But Dad was in a prison camp in Wales with other Volunteers who had been taken prisoner after the Easter Rising.

Although it was three months ago, Emer remembered it all vividly: Dad leaving home to fight with the rebels in City Hall, her begging for information about his whereabouts after he was injured and arrested, and the aftermath of the Rising, with her father lying wounded in a military hospital while she – their only child – helped Mam to run the family's two grocery shops.

It had been a difficult time, with the centre of Dublin in ruins, hundreds of people dead, and much of the population angry with the rebels for the mayhem that had been unleashed. The public mood had changed, however, after the British authorities executed sixteen of the leaders of the Rising. Lately there was more respect for the sacrifices of people like Dad, which pleased Emer. For now, though, she had to carry on without him, so she smiled at Mrs Andrews and said, 'How can I help you?'

Mrs Andrews ignored the question and pointed at the black armband that Emer had attached to the sleeve of her blouse. 'I see you're in mourning.'

'Well … not family mourning. It's for Roger Casement.'

Mrs Andrews's face tightened in distaste. The diplomat Roger Casement had been hanged by the British yesterday for his part in trying to import German arms into Ireland the week before the Rising. 'I won't be served by someone glorifying a traitor,' she said.

'He's not a traitor, Mrs Andrews,' answered Emer politely. 'He's an Irishman who died for Ireland.'

'He committed treason. Siding with Germany while we're at war.'

Emer was about to protest but stopped herself. She knew that for many Irish families with men fighting in the British Army, the Rising seemed like treachery. And although she completely disagreed, she could still respect their beliefs, especially after the terrible losses suffered by Irish regiments at the recent Battle of the Somme.

'I don't want to argue, Mrs Andrews,' said Emer. 'Can we agree to differ?'

'No, we can't. You're lucky to still have my business after your father's actions. Now take that ribbon off while you serve me.'

Emer hesitated. Mam, who also wore an armband, was in the storeroom at the back of the shop. But Emer didn't want to go scurrying to her mother. Instead she answered reasonably. 'I'm sorry, Mrs Andrews, but I'm wearing this out of respect for my father – Casement was a hero to him.'

'Then more fool your father!'

Emer felt a stab of anger, but she answered quietly. 'My father's not a fool.'

'I'm not arguing with a child. Take the ribbon off if you want my business.'

Emer was starting in secondary school next month and resented being called a child. But much as she wanted to tell Mrs Andrews what to do with her business, she wasn't sure what Mam would say if she lost them a customer.

'Don't try my patience, girl!' snapped Mrs Andrews.

'Is something the matter?'

Emer looked round to see her mother approaching.

'I won't be served by someone mourning a traitor,' said Mrs Andrews.

'I tried to explain, Mam,' said Emer, 'that Dad admires Roger Casement, and we're wearing the bands to respect both of them.'

'Your daughter has too much to say for herself, Mrs

Davey. I've already stretched a point in shopping here despite your husband's views. If you want to keep my custom, you'll both remove the armbands.'

Emer looked at her mother, whose face was slightly flushed.

'I won't have you passing judgement on my daughter, Mrs Andrews. Nor on my husband. And while we value your custom, you don't decide what we wear.'

Emer felt like cheering. She could see that Mrs Andrews was taken aback.

'In that case, I'll bid you good day!' Mrs Andrews said.

'Good day, then,' answered Mam, but already the other woman was marching towards the door.

Emer looked at her mother in awe. Six months ago, Mam would never have been so bold. But the Rising had changed their world, and now her mother was less cautious.

'Well done, Mam!' Emer said proudly. 'Well done!'

＊ ＊ ＊

Gerry smiled at his boss as their horse and cart made its way down Sackville Street. 'Hey, Mr Mac, why couldn't the pirate play cards?'

'I don't know, son, why?'

'He was sitting on the deck!'

'You're a comical lad,' said Mr Mac, cracking his whip. 'A comical lad!'

Gerry sat back happily as the horse clip-clopped over the cobblestones. He had never thought of himself as comical, but Mr Mac liked him and was easy-going, which made Gerry more relaxed than when he had worked on the slop cart with Uncle Pat.

While working with his uncle after leaving school, Gerry had applied to lots of delivery companies around the city for a job as a carter's assistant, and he still couldn't believe his luck to have landed a post with Wilson & Sons. Uncle Pat had been annoyed at first, but he had changed tack once Gerry started to hand up a weekly pay packet. Wilson's men worked long hours and the salary was modest enough, but Gerry enjoyed it much more than working for Uncle Pat.

'God, Gerry, will poor aul' Dublin ever be the same?' asked Mr Mac now, as they went past the shell of the burnt-out GPO.

'Who knows, Mr Mac?' answered Gerry.

Mr MacKeon was a plump Dubliner of about fifty, with a nasal voice and a ready laugh, and every time they drove down Sackville Street he made the same comment about the ruined buildings. But in the three months since the Rising, the rubble had been cleared from the streets, and Gerry had heard there were plans to rebuild the parts of the city centre that had been destroyed by shelling.

'Whoa there, Betsy!' cried Mr Mac after the cart turned onto the north quays. They came to a halt outside Murray's Ship Chandlers. There was a hint of salt on the warm breeze coming in from the bay, and Gerry jumped down happily and began helping Mr Mac to carry in a delivery of tarred ropes. It was their last job before lunchtime, and Gerry was looking forward to his Friday treat of fish and chips.

Mr Mac got his delivery docket signed by one of the Murray's clerks. Gerry was wondering whether he would choose cod or ray when he became aware that the clerk was staring at him. His heart suddenly lurched. It was the red-haired man he had almost knocked off the bicycle during the Rising, as he was running off with the looted clothes. He swallowed hard as the man held his gaze. Gerry quickly looked away, but it was too late. With a deep unease, he knew that he had been recognised.

CHAPTER TWO

EMER'S MIND WAS RACING as she headed for her secret meeting. She left her house on Ellesmere Avenue and crossed the North Circular Road. She turned into Prussia Street, the smell of animals and dung carrying on the summer evening air as she skirted the pens of the cattle market. She passed the stone steps of the City Arms Hotel and wondered again what the big mystery was.

A note had been put through her letter box, asking her to come alone and without telling anybody to the Prussia Street gate of the sprawling cattle market. Now as she arrived at the entrance, she saw her friend Gerry Quinn standing out of sight inside the gate.

'Emer, you came,' he said.

'How could I not, after getting a letter like that?!' she said with a smile.

Gerry didn't smile in return, and Emer stepped closer on seeing his worried look. 'What is it?'

He breathed out slowly, as though unsure where to

begin. 'Remember when you stayed in my place during the Rising?'

'Of course.' As if she would ever forget it. Gerry used to go to school with Emer's neighbour Jack, so she had known him a little bit. Despite not being close friends, Gerry had done her a big favour by letting her sleep in his room on the first night of the Rising, when Emer was afraid to return home in case the families of Volunteers would be arrested.

At the time Emer had been shocked by the poverty in Gerry's run-down cottage near the River Tolka. But despite the differences in their family backgrounds, the Rising had brought them together, and they had become friends.

'Remember the next morning, we argued about stuff I took in town?'

'Yes.' Even though Emer had been hugely grateful to Gerry for letting her stay, she had disapproved of his looting.

'I'm in trouble over it now. I need your help.'

'Anything, Gerry. What's the problem?'

'I could lose my job. And I love working with Mr Mac. It's much nicer than the slop cart and Uncle Pat.'

'Why would you lose your job?' asked Emer.

'We were doing a delivery last week. The clerk who

signed for the order recognised me. He … he seen me during the looting.'

'And you think he'll report you?'

Gerry nodded. 'He spoke to me yesterday when Mr Mac wasn't looking. He said if I don't pay him money he'll tell and I'll be sacked. Maybe arrested too.'

'But … that's blackmail!'

'I know what it is, Emer!'

'Sorry … sorry, I just … Could you get your uncle to talk to him?'

'Are you mad? Uncle Pat would just give me a hiding. No, I need to pay this fella off. Can you lend me two shillings?'

'I … I don't have it.'

'I'm really stuck, Emer.'

'I get sixpence a week pocket money. You can have that.'

'That's only a quarter of what I need. And I've got to have it by Monday. Can you … can you get some money from the shop?'

Emer was shocked. 'Oh Gerry, I can't. It would be like stealing from Mam.'

'I'll pay you back, I swear it! Just borrow it from the till for now. Please, Emer, I'm desperate.'

Emer looked at his anguished face and felt awful.

'I'll do anything else, Gerry, *anything*. But I can't steal from Mam. I'm sorry, I just can't.'

'Forget it!' shouted Gerry, his expression hardening. 'Rich people – you're all the same!'

'No, Gerry …'

'Yes! People like me don't count. I thought you were different. But you're not – you're all the same!'

Gerry turned away, and Emer felt tears welling up as she watched him storm off.

CHAPTER THREE

'DO YOU WANT to hear a good riddle?' asked Gladys.

'No. Give our brains a rest!' said her brother Ben.

'Emer, you'd like to hear it, wouldn't you?' persisted Gladys.

'Yes, all right,' answered Emer as she sat on the grassy bank of the Tolka in the hot August sunshine.

She had come to the swimming hole with her regular gang of Jack Madigan, Joan Lawlor, and Ben and Gladys Walton, but she found it hard to match their carefree mood. She was still mulling over last night's incident with Gerry.

'What goes through towns, up and over hills, but never moves?' asked Gladys.

'Your backside when we're in Dad's car!' cried Ben.

'Don't be so rude!' said Gladys.

'So what's the answer?' queried Joan.

'A road.'

'A road?' Ben looked at his sister. 'That's a hopeless riddle!'

'I don't know,' said Jack. 'I think it's kind of clever.'

'Come on!' said Joan, suddenly standing up. 'Forget about riddles and let's swim. Last one in is a rotten egg!'

Joan ran to the water's edge, gave her customary cry of 'Gang way!' and leaped in. Ben and Gladys followed, their bickering forgotten as they jumped into the sparkling water. Emer stayed sitting, and to her surprise, so did Jack. He turned to her.

'What's wrong?' he asked.

'Is it that obvious?'

'Not to everyone, but nothing escapes the eye of Sherlock Holmes!'

Although he was joking, Emer could tell that he was concerned too, and she was touched. He was a good friend, and they had become really close in the last year. It had started the previous summer, when she had saved him from drowning right here in the Tolka river. Then an even deeper bond had been forged between them when Jack's policeman father had been kidnapped by rebels during the Rising, and Emer had risked her life to help him escape.

'I was told something in secret,' said Emer, 'so I can't tell you the details.'

'Just tell me what you can then,' suggested Jack.

'I really want to help someone who's in trouble. But

to fix things, I'd have to do something wrong. And two wrongs don't make a right, do they?'

Jack shrugged. 'Depends.'

'On what?'

'The thing at stake. Ever since the Rising, I've … I've seen that things aren't always cut and dried.'

'So two wrongs *could* make a right?'

'Maybe not exactly. But sometimes a small wrong could be … what do they call it … the lesser of two evils?'

'Jack! Emer! Come on in!' cried Ben as he splashed about with the others.

'Coming!' called Jack, then he turned back to Emer. 'Does that make any sense?'

'Yeah,' she answered with a nod. 'Yeah. Go on, have your swim.'

'Aren't you coming?'

'No,' said Emer. 'No, I need to think …'

CHAPTER FOUR

'NO EXCUSES! Just give me the money.'

Gerry felt his hatred for the blackmailer rising, but he forced himself to stay calm. They were meeting at lunchtime in a smelly laneway behind the shell-damaged Wynn's Hotel, not far from Murray's Ship Chandlers.

Gerry had discovered that the clerk's name was Thomas Byrne. He was a clean-shaven man in his mid-twenties with close-cropped ginger hair, and he spoke with the accent of a Dubliner who was trying to sound posher than he was. Even without the blackmail, Gerry would have disliked him, but he knew he had to handle Byrne carefully.

'There's one and six there,' Gerry said, passing over the coins. 'It's all I could get.'

'I said two shillings.'

'I couldn't raise two. You only told me on Friday.'

Byrne stared at Gerry, his expression calculating. 'What do you earn each week? And don't lie!'

'Seven shillings and sixpence,' answered Gerry

reluctantly. 'But my pocket money is just a shilling – my uncle gets the rest.'

'He'll have to take less while you pay for your crime.'

'What?'

'You probably stole at least five pounds' worth of stuff. You need to pay that back to society.' Byrne gave a humourless smile. 'With me acting for society.'

'Look–'

'Don't interrupt. You'll pay two shillings a week, and after a year we'll wipe the slate clean.'

'How can I give you two shillings when all I get is one?'

Byrne shrugged. 'Negotiate more pocket money. Work overtime. Get a pay rise. I don't actually care.'

'Please. I can give you one shilling a week.'

'Two. Or if you'd prefer, don't pay me at all. We can call the police. You won't have to worry about money then – you'll go to a reformatory. And I hear they're *really* nice.'

Gerry had heard horror stories about reformatory schools. His stomach tightened.

'So, what's it to be?'

'I'll … I'll pay you.'

'Good. Two shillings a week from next payday.' Byrne smiled. 'I'll write off the missing sixpence this week as a goodwill gesture.' He suddenly grabbed Gerry by the shirt and pulled him close. 'But don't *ever* make the mistake of thinking I'm soft. Got it?'

'Yeah.'

'Right,' said Byrne, releasing Gerry. 'See you next Friday.'

He walked away, and Gerry stood alone in the laneway, trying to fight off a wave of despair.

✳ ✳ ✳

'Why can't we just tell Dad the truth?' asked Emer as she put down her cup and looked at her mother across the kitchen table. It was six o'clock, and the evening sunshine bathed the room in a warm glow while they finished their tea.

'We *can* tell Dad what's happening. We just need to … to phrase it carefully,' answered her mother.

They had just received a letter from Frongoch prison camp in Wales, where Emer's father was being held with other Volunteers including Michael Collins and Arthur Griffith. The good news was that Dad's shattered leg was healing well and that he had won a chess tournament organised by the prisoners. But her father had asked how their two grocery shops were doing, and Mam had been reluctant to report that profits had increased. Since

Emer and Mam had taken over the business, they had run it more efficiently than her distracted father had in the months leading up to the Rising.

'I'd say Dad would be delighted we're doing well,' suggested Emer.

'Yes, but he's still a man.'

'What does that mean?'

'He has his pride. He's used to being in charge – we don't want to undermine him.'

'So because we're not men, we pretend to be dimmer than we are?'

'You don't always have to be so feisty, Emer. We'll tell Dad that business is good, but without rubbing his nose in it.'

Emer thought this was a silly approach, but she said nothing, not wanting to argue with her mother tonight. In truth she felt slightly guilty, knowing that she was about to do something Mam wouldn't like.

'May I leave the table?' she asked.

'Yes, you may.'

Emer pushed back her chair, slipped a table knife up her sleeve and exited to the hall. She quickly ascended the stairs to her room, closing the door after her. Dropping to her knees, she reached under her bed and took out a charity collector's box.

She had been saving for a new bicycle for the last few months, and Mam had agreed to match whatever Emer saved. The box – which couldn't readily be opened – had been Mam's idea, to help Emer resist the temptation of dipping into a normal piggy bank. But Emer had heard that you could slide money out of a collector's box with a flat-bladed knife.

She stared at the box and thought again about Gerry. She couldn't change the whole world, but she could help a friend in need if she took Jack's advice on the lesser of two evils. She would be breaking a deal made with Mam if she raided the box, which was why it hadn't occurred to her when Gerry had asked for money. But the cash was *hers* – it wasn't like she was stealing from the shop. Still Emer hesitated. Then she recalled Gerry's anguished face, and before she could lose her nerve she lifted the box, slid the knife into the hole and carefully began extracting the money.

✳ ✳ ✳

'Bring a bucket of oats to Daisy,' ordered Uncle Pat as he sat at the table, pouring himself a large tumbler of whiskey.

Gerry was relaxing in the shabby armchair at the fireplace, carving a stick of wood with his penknife.

'Can I do it in a few minutes?' he asked. 'Mr Mac and I had a really tiring day.'

'Do it when I say, you lazy pup!'

'All right,' Gerry said wearily, knowing it was better not to argue with Pat when he was drinking.

He rose from the armchair and crossed the room, then stepped out of the cottage. The Tolka Valley looked beautiful in the evening sunlight, Gerry thought as he made for the dilapidated shed where supplies were kept for Daisy, his uncle's horse. Rounding the corner, he came to a sudden halt as Emer stepped out from the nearby trees.

'Emer! What are you—'

'I had to see you,' she interrupted. 'I got you some money.' She held up a small pouch of coins. 'It's almost two shillings. It will buy you some time.'

Gerry didn't know what to say. He felt his cheeks flush with embarrassment as he remembered how he had called Emer rich and uncaring the other day at the cattle market.

'I didn't have to take it from the shop,' explained Emer. 'It was my savings towards a new bike, so it won't be missed for a while.'

Gerry was touched that she would give up her savings after how he had treated her, and he felt a lump in his throat.

'God, Emer, I … I don't know what to say.'

'Don't say anything, just take it.' She reached out and pushed the pouch of coins into his hand.

Gerry looked at her, trying to keep his emotions in check. 'I'm … I'm really sorry for what I said.'

Emer touched his arm. 'It's all right, Gerry.'

'No. No, it's not all right. I'm … I'm … '

'What?' asked Emer gently.

'I'm just so sorry. You're dead sound, Emer.'

To his surprise, he saw that her eyes began to well up. 'Thanks, Gerry,' she said softly.

They looked at each other, and for a second he wanted to hug her. But he knew that would feel awkward, so instead he gave a wry smile. 'Well … dead sound for a posh girl.'

Emer smiled back. 'I'll settle for that.' She held out her hand. 'Friends again?'

Gerry nodded and shook her hand. 'Friends again,' he said.

CHAPTER FIVE

'Can I have a ton of potatoes and one carrot, please?' said Jack with a straight face.

Emer was serving behind the counter of the grocery shop and she laughed, then asked her friend, 'What brings you here?'

'I was passing, and I thought I'd brighten up your morning. Your mam's not here, is she?'

'No, she won't be back for an hour.'

'Good. Don't want to get blamed for distracting you.'

'Distract away.'

'OK, I heard this fruit joke, and seeing as you sell fruit and vegetables …'

'Why do I know this will be bad?'

'So, what do you call two banana peels?'

'What *do* you call two banana peels?' asked Emer.

'A pair of slippers!'

'I knew it would be terrible.'

'But you're laughing.'

'That's more out of pity!'

Emer was glad to see Jack. She suspected the real

reason he had called in was that she had been subdued when they went swimming at the Tolka, and he was concerned for her. Looking him in the eye, she dropped the jokey tone. 'Thanks for the advice on Sunday – about the lesser of two evils.'

'Did it help?'

Emer nodded. 'Yes, it did, I …'

'What?'

Emer hesitated. She hadn't shared Gerry's secret with anyone, but keeping it to herself was a strain. And Jack was completely trustworthy. 'If I tell you something, can we keep it strictly between ourselves?'

'Of course.'

Emer took a deep breath, then with a sense of relief she told the story of the blackmail.

'That's awful!' said Jack.

'Yeah, poor Gerry.'

'I meant the whole thing, Emer. It's awful too that Gerry looted.'

'That's what I thought at first. We argued about it when I stayed in his house. But his answer was that he's been hungry and cold too often – and just once in his life he got a break.'

Jack nodded reluctantly. 'I suppose there is that.'

'The real villain is the blackmailer.'

'Absolutely. He should be arrested.'

'But then it would come out about Gerry, and he'd lose his job. He might even be sent away to a reformatory school.'

'Yeah.'

'I don't know what's right, Jack. I gave Gerry money to buy him time. But now I'm thinking – is that just encouraging blackmail?'

'No, I think you did right.'

'Really?' asked Emer, relieved.

'Yes. But …' Jack breathed out. 'But how do you stop it?'

'That's what I keep asking myself. And so far … I don't have an answer.'

✳   ✳   ✳

The August sun beat down from a clear blue sky, and the Friday lunchtime crowds were good humoured, giving Dublin a relaxed, holiday feel. Gerry turned in off the quays, heading for the lane behind Wynn's Hotel. The heat made the place smell worse than usual, and Gerry wrinkled his nose, the scent of rotting food reminding him of Uncle Pat's slop cart.

As he continued on, he ran his tongue over the last piece of toffee that was stuck to his teeth, savouring the sweet, sticky taste. He had bought a halfpenny worth of throwouts – chocolate toffees that were factory rejects – as a payday treat to cheer himself up after a bad week.

Having pooled all his pocket money with the cash from Emer, he had enough to pay Thomas Byrne this time. And if his plan succeeded, he mightn't have to pay him ever again.

He made his way along the lane and from an open window heard somebody playing a piano. The song was 'Keep the Home Fires Burning', and the haunting war-time tune seemed at odds with the summer atmosphere. But war news was never far away. Gerry had just seen in a newspaper that British casualties continued to be catastrophic in the aftermath of last month's Battle of the Somme, in which they had suffered staggering losses. The sad air of the song made him feel sorry for the soldiers at the front – but then he saw Byrne approaching and immediately forgot everything else.

Gerry walked towards the blackmailer, deliberately making his stride seem confident – he knew that if he were to carry off his plan, he mustn't show any weakness.

'If it's not my looter friend,' said Byrne with his usual humourless smile. 'I take it you have my money?'

Gerry stopped and looked him in the eye. 'It's not *your* money, it's *my* money.'

'For about five more seconds. And this time you better have the full two shillings.'

Gerry reached into his pocket and took out a pouch of coins. 'I have the full two shillings, but–'

'But? There's no "but". You'll have two shillings this week, and every week.'

'No,' said Gerry firmly. He tossed the pouch to Byrne, who managed to catch it despite being taken by surprise.

'You got one and six for last week,' said Gerry, 'and now two shillings more. That's all you're getting, and if you're smart you'll quit while you're ahead.'

'Who the hell do you think you're talking to?!'

'A criminal,' answered Gerry coolly. 'You're black-mailing me for breaking the law. But blackmail is a crime too. You could end up arrested yourself.'

Byrne looked angry, and Gerry steeled himself to fight back if the other man struck out. Instead Byrne spoke in a cold, flat voice. 'So what are you going to do? Tell the police you were a looter?'

'I won't say anything – provided you don't. But if you squeal, I'll tell them everything, and we'll both be for it.'

'Wrong. *You'll* be for it. Before you know it, you'll

be in a reformatory. They'll beat you black and blue in there, and no-one will lift a finger to stop it.'

Gerry tried not to let his fear show and continued to speak defiantly. 'Maybe you won't have such a good time yourself in jail.'

'Except I won't be in jail. I'll deny everything. And you'll be seen as a little slum rat trying to blacken the name of a decent citizen.'

'No …'

'Yes! Look at yourself. Look at your clothes, listen to your accent, look at your job. That's what the police will do. Then look at me: a well-dressed, well-spoken clerk in a respectable firm. Who do you think they'll believe?'

Gerry couldn't come up with a convincing reply.

'*Everyone* will believe me. *No-one* will believe you.' Byrne pointed his finger aggressively. 'Same place next Friday. Don't come without the money.'

Byrne walked off and Gerry stood unmoving, desperately trying to figure out what to do next.

CHAPTER SIX

'Mixing ice cream and lemonade – whoever thought that up was a genius!' declared Joan.

'Amen to that,' said Ben, moving his straw around the bottom of his glass and slurping up the delicious mixture.

'Do you have to sound like a pig?' asked Gladys.

'Do you have to look like one?' he answered back.

'Ben! That's not very nice!' said Emer, although she knew this was just the way the siblings sparred, and that there was no malice involved.

It was a sunny Sunday afternoon, and the friends were in the Madigans' back garden, where Jack's mother had served up the ice cream and lemonade. The back window was left open so that they could hear the gramophone, and Emer was enjoying the lazy summer atmosphere as she hummed along to 'Hello, Hawaii, How Are You?'

'I like that song,' said Jack, 'but doesn't the ukulele sound … I don't know … kind of silly?'

'I love the ukulele!' said Joan. 'It sounds like the

kind of thing you'd play when you're in good humour.'

'It's just another craze,' suggested Emer, 'like the tango a few years ago.'

'Yeah,' agreed Jack, 'but the tango was better.'

Joan grinned. 'Except people looked *daft* when they were dancing to it!'

'I think "If You Were the Only Girl in the World" is the best new song in ages,' said Gladys.

Ben snorted. 'Dead soppy!'

'Well, thousands of people bought it,' his sister answered.

Emer nodded in agreement. 'Whoever wrote that must be making a fortune. Imagine earning a living writing songs.'

'People get money in ways you'd never think of,' said Joan with a knowing air.

Jack looked at her with interest. 'Like what?'

'The insurance company where Dad works got big claims for damage during the Rising. Some people want *huge* payouts.'

'And a fortune will be spent rebuilding the city,' added Ben. 'Our dad's firm is going to tender for some of the electrical work.'

'There you are,' said Joan. 'Every cloud has a silver lining.'

Jack put down his glass. 'It's not much of a silver lining to the people killed because of the rebellion.'

Even though Jack was her friend, Emer felt her hackles rising. 'It wasn't the rebels who shelled the city centre, Jack. It was British artillery. And the army did it even though they knew thousands of people lived there.'

'The rebels knew that too,' retorted Jack. 'But it didn't stop them occupying the centre of Dublin, did it?'

Emer was about to argue, but Joan raised her hands to both of them. 'No more aul' politics! Let's play another record,' she suggested as the song on the gramophone ended.

Jack hesitated, then nodded. 'OK.'

'Emer?'

Because their families had taken opposing sides during the Rising – with Emer and her father on the rebel side and Jack's dad out with the Dublin Metropolitan Police – Emer and Jack normally avoided talking about politics. Already Emer regretted this flare-up, and besides, they had decided to work together to help Gerry. 'Yeah,' she agreed, 'OK.'

She returned her attention to her ice cream as Jack went inside to play another record. But now her mind had shifted to Gerry, who, even on his Sunday off, had to do jobs for his uncle. She really wanted to help him, and she wondered, yet again, how they could stop the blackmail.

CHAPTER SEVEN

GERRY FELT NERVOUS as he approached Davey's grocery shop. He needed to talk to Emer but was afraid that her mother might also be serving. He had never met Mrs Davey, but he had the impression from Emer that she was formidable.

He was on his lunch break, and Mr Mac had dropped him off near Davey's Bolton Street branch. It was three days now since his unsuccessful bid to bluff Thomas Byrne, and he had spent the weekend mulling over his problem before finally coming up with a plan. To make it work, though, he would need help.

Gerry stood on the sunlit pavement for a moment, getting up his nerve, then he stepped forward and entered the shop. Despite the summer heat, it was shady and cool inside. Gerry saw Emer at the far end laying out a shining display of polished apples. Before he could greet her, he became aware of a well-dressed woman behind the counter. She looked like an older, more serious version of Emer, and he knew that it had to be Mrs Davey.

The woman was watching him closely. Gerry knew that look. *She's afraid I'm here to steal something.* Admittedly he was in his threadbare work clothes, but it was still unsettling to be regarded with such suspicion.

'May I help you?' she asked.

'I just came in to see Emer.'

Hearing his voice, Emer quickly approached, looking surprised but pleased. 'Gerry!'

'Emer.'

'Mam, this is Gerry Quinn. Gerry's the boy who let me stay in his house the first night of the Rising!'

'Oh,' said Mrs Davey, unable to mask her surprise. 'Well, thank you for offering Emer shelter.' She held out her hand to Gerry.

'It was nothing,' said Gerry, shaking hands. He could see that Mrs Davey wanted to ask him what he was doing there, and he felt uneasy. 'I just … I wanted to see Emer again. To tell her about Daisy.'

Mrs Davey raised an eyebrow. 'Daisy?'

'Gerry's horse,' explained Emer. 'She was … she was expecting a foal. Can I be excused for a few minutes, Mam?'

'Yes, of course.'

'We'll pop outside, Gerry,' said Emer.

Gerry was relieved by her intervention, and he

turned to Mrs Davey. 'Nice meeting you.'

'My pleasure. And thank you again for your kindness to Emer.'

Gerry nodded in farewell, thinking that while her words were polite, there was a slight coolness to her manner.

They stepped out onto the busy thoroughfare of Bolton Street, and Emer guided Gerry to a quieter laneway several yards away from the shop. 'Has something happened?' she asked excitedly.

'Yeah. I tried to threaten Byrne, but it didn't work.'

'Really?'

'He said he'd just deny everything and that nobody would believe me. And he's right. I should have known no-one would take my side.'

'*I'm* on your side.'

'Sorry, I didn't mean it like that.'

'I know. And actually … there's someone else on your side too.'

'Who?'

'Jack.'

'You told Jack?'

'I'm sorry, Gerry, but I had to tell someone – the strain was killing me. But Jack won't say a word, and he'll help if he can. Is that OK?'

Her obvious sincerity made it impossible to be annoyed. 'OK,' he said.

'So where does that leave you with Byrne?'

'He's still demanding two shillings this Friday – and every Friday for the next year. I haven't even got it for this week.'

'Well, with your pocket money, my pocket money and Jack's pocket money, we can probably cover this Friday,' said Emer.

'That would be great. Because … I've made a plan.'

'What sort of plan?'

'The following Friday, once I get my week's wages, I'm running away.'

'What?!'

'I have to, Emer. I can't raise two bob each week, and I can't keep trying to buy time. He's going to end up turning me in. I'll be sent to a hellhole like Letterfrack, and I can't … I can't face that, Emer. I just can't.'

'OK, Gerry, OK,' she said, squeezing his arm sympathetically. 'So … what's your plan?'

'If I make it to England, I could vanish there.'

'England?'

'There's loads of work because of the war. I'm good with horses – I could work in a stable or a blacksmiths.'

'What about your uncle?'

'All he cares about is drinking.'

'But you won't be allowed to travel on your own. And you don't know anyone in England. Supposing you don't get a job because you're too young?'

'I *will* get a job. And if I'm really stuck, I'll sign up as a boy soldier. I've jumped up in height this year, so I'll just lie about my age.'

'I don't know, Gerry …'

'I can't go to Letterfrack! I've heard the stories, Emer. I can't go there!'

'OK, OK.'

'I haven't worked it all out, but I've got to get on the Liverpool ferry. That's why I came to see you. Will you … will you help me escape?'

She held his gaze, then nodded. 'Yes, I will.'

Gerry breathed out slowly. 'Thanks, Emer,' he said. 'That really means a lot.'

* * *

'Well, that was … unexpected,' said Mam.

Emer had come back into the shop, and she picked up on the note of disapproval in her mother's voice. She knew that Mam wasn't simply referring to Gerry's visit; the unspoken notion was that Emer being involved with someone of Gerry's class was also unexpected.

Emer felt disappointed. Her mother had always been conscious of appearances and doing what was 'proper', but after the upheaval of the Rising she felt that Mam had become more open in her thinking, more willing to accept change. She had been proud when her mother had stood up to Mrs Andrews. But looking down on Gerry seemed ungrateful and snobbish, and Emer had to resist the temptation to give a smart answer.

'He has very little, Mam,' she said evenly. 'But when I was in trouble, he shared the little he had.'

To her mother's credit, she looked embarrassed. 'Yes, well, that's … that's certainly admirable.'

'I think it is,' said Emer. 'Now I'd better get back to the apples.'

Emer made for the rear of the shop, putting her mother's reaction from her mind. Her head was reeling with the enormity of Gerry running away from home, but she forced herself to focus, and she began thinking about how to help him escape.

CHAPTER EIGHT

'SEE YOU, MR MAC!' cried Gerry, forcing himself to sound cheery as he jumped down from the cart onto the pavement. They were finished their deliveries for the day, and Gerry was about to walk home while his boss returned the horse and cart to the stables of Wilson & Sons. Mr Mac smiled at Gerry and gave a playful salute before clip-clopping away.

Gerry began walking towards Phibsboro, torn between anxiety over his escape plans and sadness at the idea of leaving Mr Mac behind. He had grown really fond of the good-humoured carter, and he wished that instead of having Uncle Pat as his guardian, he could have had someone kind like Mr Mac.

As if to illustrate the difference between them, this morning his uncle had thumped him for forgetting to steep their porridge the night before, whereas Mr Mac had brought him two thick slices of apple tart that his wife had baked.

Gerry was looking forward to getting away from Uncle Pat, but he resented having to flee his native city.

He had made one last attempt to convince Thomas Byrne that the weekly payment was too much when they had met at lunchtime today at the Custom House. Byrne had decided that they should vary the places where they met, but he had flatly rejected Gerry's appeal. 'Two shillings is the agreed rate,' he had insisted.

Gerry had tried to control his anger. '*Agreed*?'

'Agreed by me. And I'm tired of your whining. Complain again and I'll raise it to half a crown.'

'Ye robber! You're more a thief than I ever was!' snapped Gerry.

'Don't give me lip, you brat! Don't you dare!'

'Why? 'Cause you wear a collar and tie and you're a clerk? Who are you to look down on me?!'

'*Anyone* could look down on you! What are you? A looter, a slum rat, a cornerboy who should be thanking his stars someone gave him a job! But if you don't want your job, if you'd rather be arrested, we can arrange that. We can arrange it right now. How about I drag you by the scruff of the neck to Store Street police station?'

Gerry bunched his fists and drew himself up to his full height. 'I'd like to see you try.'

Byrne stared hard at him, but Gerry held his gaze. After a moment, Byrne shook his head. 'I won't make a spectacle of myself on a public street.'

Gerry felt a surge of triumph. His victory was short-lived, though, and Byrne's next words chilled him. 'No need to take you to the police station. I'll just report you and let the police drag you off screaming. Good practice for the reformatory. You'll do plenty of screaming there.'

Gerry felt a jolt of fear and realised that he had to retrieve the situation. *What had he been thinking?* He needed to keep Byrne sweet for one more week if he was to get away to Liverpool.

'All right,' he said quietly. 'All right, here's the two bob.' He held out the money. Byrne said nothing, and Gerry felt his heart pounding. *Please God,* he thought, *let him take it.*

The silence seemed to last forever, but finally Byrne spoke. 'I should really make it half a crown for all your mouthing off.'

'Please,' said Gerry, 'I don't have half a crown. Take the two shillings – and I'll have it next week as well.'

'And every other week. No more lip, no more quibbling. Understood?'

'Understood,' said Gerry, passing over the cash.

That had all happened at lunchtime, and Gerry was still angry now as he walked down Prospect Road toward the Tolka. But by appearing to back down from

Byrne, he had bought himself time – and a week from now he would make his escape bid. It would be risky and unpredictable, but somehow he had to get away. Wishing it could be sooner, he quickened his pace and made for home.

❋ ❋ ❋

Emer watched from the front window as Jack's parents walked arm-in-arm down Ellesmere Avenue. She waited until they were almost out of sight, then she swiftly made her way out the front door and up the road to Jack's house. Mr and Mrs Madigan were dressed in their Sunday clothes. Presumably they were going to visit family or friends, and Emer was determined to take her chance while they were out. She felt nervous, but she forced herself to be calm as she knocked on the hall door.

After a moment, Jack appeared and smiled welcomingly. 'Emer, come on in.'

'Thanks,' she said, stepping into the hall. 'Are your sisters here?'

'Just Maureen.'

'Can we talk somewhere private?'

Jack indicated a doorway off the hall. 'Come into the parlour.'

Emer entered the Madigans' front room, then turned to face her friend.

'What's happened?' Jack asked.

'I spoke to Gerry. He made one last try with the blackmailer.'

'But it didn't work?'

Emer shook her head. 'So he's going to make his break next Friday. On the evening ferry to Liverpool.'

'I can't believe this is really happening.'

'I know, it's awful,' said Emer. 'But we've been through all that. Getting to England's his best hope.'

'Right.'

Emer hesitated, almost afraid to reveal why she was paying this visit. 'You're … you're still on to help Gerry?'

'Of course.'

'I'm glad to hear it, Jack. Because I need you to do something, and …'

'What?'

Emer held his gaze but spoke reluctantly. 'And you're not going to like it.'

* * *

Gerry thought he would scream if Uncle Pat sang 'Wait Till the Sun Shines, Nellie' one more time. His uncle kept drunkenly singing the same line at intervals as he sat at their battered dinner table, a bottle of *poitín* in his hand. Pat had spent the afternoon in a local pub and was now at the maudlin stage of drunkenness that Gerry hated.

Gerry wished that Pat's so-called friends wouldn't provide him with spirits when it was obvious that he couldn't handle alcohol. But the *poitín* had been in payment for a favour Pat had done, and Gerry suspected that he would work his way through the whole bottle before the night was over.

'Do you know what I'm going to tell you, Gerry?' he said now.

'No.'

'You're not the worst … You're not the worst, Gerry.'

'Right.'

'Family comes first, that's what I say. I could have let you go to an orphanage, but no, I took you in!' said Pat proudly.

Gerry felt like pointing out that he had more than paid his way, working hard on the slop cart and now giving Pat most of his wages, but he said nothing.

'I took you in, and hasn't it worked out great for both of us?'

'Has it?' said Gerry, the words slipping out before he could stop himself.

His uncle's senses had been dulled by the drink, but Pat's face clouded now as he slowly responded to Gerry's answer. 'What … what are you saying?'

Gerry wanted to reply that living with a drunk who beat him whenever he lost his temper wasn't all that great. But if he did, he risked another explosion from his uncle, who could go from sentimental to violent very quickly.

'What do you mean by that?' asked Pat again, his tone challenging.

Gerry was fed up humouring him and desperately wanted to speak the truth, but he forced himself not to. He had to keep things normal until Friday. If he could escape to England, he wouldn't have to put up with any more of this.

'I just meant … were you happy with me in the new job,' said Gerry, improvising. 'It's worked out, hasn't it, having the regular pay?'

'Indeed and it has!' said Pat happily, his aggressive air suddenly replaced by maudlin affection. 'Me aul' sego-sha!' he said, tossing Gerry's hair. 'You're a good little worker.'

Gerry thought that he almost preferred it when his uncle was grumpy, but he made himself smile in return.

Pat began singing 'Wait Till the Sun Shines, Nellie'

again, and Gerry rose from the table and began clearing the dishes, counting the days until his getaway.

* * *

'Steal police notepaper?!' said Jack. 'Are you mad?!'

Emer sat forward in her chair in the Madigans' spick-and-span parlour, keeping her voice calm and reasonable. 'You told me your dad often does paperwork at home,' she said. 'He must have headed paper.'

'He does. But I can't just take it!'

Emer had expected that Jack would be shocked, and she had rehearsed her argument. 'Gerry's in an awful fix,' she said. 'If *we* don't help him, he has nowhere to turn.'

'I will help him,' said Jack. 'But don't ask me to steal from my father.'

'It's not from your father, it's from the police. And it's not really stealing – it's just one sheet of paper.'

'That's splitting hairs, Emer.'

'Maybe. But it could make all the difference to Gerry.'

Jack started to object, but Emer held up her hand. 'Just hear me out, Jack, please.'

'All right,' he said reluctantly.

'Look, the weakest link in Gerry's plan is getting onto the ferry. We know the police watch who comes in and out of the country, so a boy travelling without an adult could easily be stopped and questioned. But if he has a typed letter on police notepaper, it makes it all seem official.'

'A typed letter saying what?'

'That his father was badly wounded in the war, and that Gerry is going to England to visit him in hospital. His mother has to stay in Dublin to mind a sick child, and because Gerry is a minor, she got police permission for him to travel alone.'

'Supposing it doesn't work and the letter's traced to me? I'd be in huge trouble!'

Emer hesitated, hating what she was about to say. But Gerry had no-one else on his side – she had to enlist Jack's help. She looked him in the eye and spoke earnestly. 'I could have said the same to you, Jack, during the Rising. Except I wouldn't have just gotten into trouble – I could have been killed trying to save your father.'

Jack couldn't hold her gaze. He looked down sheepishly, then after a moment turned back to face her. 'I'll never forget that. I could never pay you back for all you did.' He nodded slowly. 'OK, I'll do it.'

'Thanks, Jack. And … it's not just one good turn deserving another. Helping Gerry out – it's the right thing to do.'

'I know. But … will the plan work?'

Emer breathed out. 'I'll be honest – there's no guarantee. But I couldn't bear not to try and help. We can't stand by while Gerry ends up in a reformatory.'

'No, we can't. All right,' said Jack decisively, 'in for a penny, in for a pound. When do you need the headed paper?'

'Can we get it now, while your dad's not here? Then I could use it in Mam's typewriter when she's out tomorrow night.'

Jack hesitated briefly, as though getting up his nerve. 'OK,' he said, 'I'll see if I can find it.'

CHAPTER NINE

GERRY LOOKED at the ruins of the GPO and waited for Mr Mac to say his piece as they headed down Sackville Street to begin their Monday deliveries.

'God, Gerry ...' he said, shaking his head.

'Will the place ever recover?' Gerry answered for him with a smile.

Mr Mac gave a wry grin. 'I suppose I do repeat meself a bit.'

'Sure if we were perfect, there'd be no room to improve!'

'Good point, Gerry! Good point!'.

As the carter flicked his whip and the horse picked up speed, Gerry felt regretful. He desperately wanted to get away on Friday, but he would miss Mr Mac and their friendly banter. And because the escape plan called for a secret departure, he wouldn't be able to thank him for his kindness or even say a proper goodbye.

The cart reached the end of Sackville Street and turned onto the quays. Gerry's pulse began to quicken as they came to a halt outside Murray's Ship Chandlers.

Thomas Byrne was usually the clerk who signed for their deliveries, and Gerry hated having to be in his presence. Sure enough, Byrne appeared as Gerry and Mr Mac carried in a delivery of canvas and tarred ropes.

'So how is this fella working out for you, Mr MacKeon?' he asked.

'Ah, sure, Gerry is a grand lad.'

'I hope he knows what a good job he has. There'd be no problem getting someone to replace him!' said Byrne with false heartiness.

'Ah no, Gerry's sound as a pound.'

'They're the ones you have to watch,' said Byrne, continuing his mock playfulness. 'You wouldn't know what crimes they'd be capable of! Amn't I right?' he said directly to Gerry.

Gerry felt his heart pounding, but he tried to look calm. *He's just playing cat and mouse*, he told himself. *He won't want to lose two shillings a week by turning me in.* But he couldn't be sure. Maybe Byrne would settle for what he had already been paid for the enjoyment of shocking Mr Mac and alerting the police.

'Don't be tormenting the young fella,' said Mr Mac, holding out the delivery docket for Byrne to sign.

'Oh, I'd say he's well able to look after himself.' Byrne quickly signed the paperwork, then looked at

Gerry again. 'Yes, *well* able to help himself.'

There was a hint of a cruel smile on Byrne's lips, and Gerry feared that he was going to refer to the looting.

'OK, we better get moving, Gerry,' said Mr Mac.

Gerry held his breath, awaiting Byrne's response.

'See you soon,' said the clerk, nodding to Mr Mac. He gave Gerry a tiny smirk before walking off towards his office.

Gerry breathed out and followed his boss to the cart.

Mr Mac paused for a moment on the busy pavement. 'There's something about that fella,' he said. 'I can't warm to him.'

'Me neither,' said Gerry. 'He's not very nice. But …'

'What?'

Gerry knew that this was the best chance he might have for a thank you or a farewell. 'But you are, Mr Mac. Really nice.'

'Ah, Gerry …'

'It's great working with you.' Gerry found his eyes welling up and he felt embarrassed. Turning away, he quickly mounted the cart, then called back over his shoulder, 'Right, let's go then …'

* * *

'"Aforementioned" is a great word,' said Jack. 'Let's try and work that in.'

'Yeah,' said Emer. 'It sounds real official.'

The evening sun warmed the kitchen of Emer's house as they sat at the table composing the letter for Gerry. Mrs Davey had gone to visit her dressmaker, and Emer had slipped the police notepaper into the typewriter that her mother used for doing the accounts.

'What about "the aforementioned boy will travel unaccompanied to Liverpool"?' suggested Emer.

Jack nodded his approval. 'Sounds good. Or maybe … maybe the "said" boy. "The said boy will travel unaccompanied on the aforementioned ferry"?'

'Perfect!' cried Emer. 'You really know the lingo.'

'Well, my dad *has* been a policeman for over twenty years.'

'OK, let me type that.' She carefully selected the correct keys and typed in the phrase. She had already typed 'To whom it may concern' on an envelope, and the letter was almost finished, based on the fiction of Gerry travelling to England to visit his wounded father.

'All right, how will we wrap it up?' asked Emer.

Jack thought for a moment. '"I thank you in anticipation of your co-operation in this matter."'

'God, Jack, you're brilliant at this!'

'We try to please.'

Emer typed in the new sentence, then awaited further instructions from her friend.

'And then just put, "Yours faithfully, Inspector Timothy Rooney, A Division." And leave a space where I can do his signature.'

'Right.' Emer typed the final words, then looked at Jack. 'Thanks for doing this, Jack. I know ... I know it was a lot to ask.'

'It's OK, I just hope—'

But before he could finish, they heard the hall door opening.

'Quick, it's Mam!' cried Emer. She pulled the sheet of paper from the typewriter and swiftly crossed the room, putting the machine back on the shelf above the dresser.

'Emer, Jack,' said her mother, entering the room.

'Mam, I ... I wasn't expecting you.'

'The dressmaker had to go to a funeral. Are you ... are you all right?'

Emer realised that she seemed flustered, and she forced herself to speak normally. 'Yes, I'm fine.' But with her mother in the way, Emer couldn't see if the headed paper lay where she had left it on the table.

She swallowed hard, knowing it would be a disaster if Mam found the forged letter.

'Isn't it awful, Mrs Davey, about the Armenians being massacred?' asked Jack, referring to last week's killings by the Ottoman Empire of thousands of Armenians. Emer recognised this as a diversion.

Although the Madigans were in the opposing camp to the Daveys politically, Emer's mother liked Jack, and she responded politely to him.

'Yes, it's dreadful,' she answered. 'I don't know what the world is coming to.'

While her mother was distracted, Emer moved towards the table, her pulses racing madly. She looked for the letter but couldn't see it. Then Jack caught her eye and gave the subtlest of winks, and she knew he must have snapped it up. She felt a huge sense of relief, and she winked in return, pleased with Jack's quick thinking and excited that their plan was still in place.

CHAPTER TEN

GERRY SNAPPED SHUT the latches on his small, battered suitcase and prepared to leave the cottage for the last time. Friday evening had finally come around, and now that he was about to make his way to the ferry, his emotions were in turmoil. Part of him was excited at the idea of a new life away from people like Thomas Byrne and Uncle Pat. But he was also frightened that the police might arrest him, and it felt strange to leave behind everyone and everything he knew.

He was wearing his best outfit, which included one of the looted shirts. He had packed into the suitcase spare clothes and his prized possessions – two medals won at football, a boys' annual that Jack had given him last Christmas, and the toy monkey he got for his sixth birthday, which was his only link back to his parents.

So far everything had gone to plan. At lunchtime he had skipped his scheduled meeting with Byrne and instead gone to buy the ferry ticket to Liverpool. Uncle Pat normally went to the pub after work on Fridays, and Gerry hoped to be at sea by the time his uncle came home later tonight. With luck, Pat would arrive back drunk and not discover that he was missing until tomorrow morning, but in case he came earlier, Gerry had a back-up plan: he had bought a bottle of cheap whiskey too. Now he entered Pat's bedroom and placed the whiskey on his pillow alongside a handwritten note. He read through it one final time.

Dear Uncle Pat,

I've had my fill of Dublin and I've got work in another part of the country. Don't come looking for me you won't find me I'm starting a new life under a different name. Here's a bottle of whiskey to help you drown your sorrows — though I know you won't miss me that much.

The one thing I'm glad about is that I wasn't put into an orphanage so thank you for that.

Your nephew,

Gerry

There was always the risk that if Pat came home early, he might report Gerry's flight to the police. But knowing his uncle, Gerry reckoned that he wouldn't be able to resist the temptation of drinking the whiskey first. All Gerry needed was to delay things so that he would be out of the country before the alarm was raised — that's if Pat raised an alarm at all, which was unlikely. Still, better to leave as little as possible to chance, Gerry thought.

He stepped out into the kitchen, took up the suitcase and made for the door. It was a bright summer evening, and he shielded his eyes as he left the gloom of the cottage. He looked up the Tolka Valley, bathed in a golden glow from the dipping sun, and felt a pang of regret to be leaving home. He gazed at the view for a moment, committing the image to his memory. Then he turned away, walking briskly towards town and the Liverpool ferry.

✳   ✳   ✳

Emer pretended to read her library book as Mam pottered about the kitchen. Her mother was late leaving for a night of bridge. She had picked up this hobby after Emer's dad had gone to prison, and now she never missed a Friday-night game. Emer glanced anxiously at the clock on the dresser, eager to make her move the moment Mam left.

The plan was that she and Jack would get the tram to town and assist Gerry in his escape bid. It all had to be kept secret from Mam, however, so Emer couldn't reveal her concern that things were running late.

Each week her mother got a lift to the bridge game in the Model T Ford that was the pride and joy of her friends Mr and Mrs Herlihy. The Herlihys lived on Blackhorse Avenue, and they collected Mam on their way into the city centre.

Why did they have to be late tonight?! Emer thought, turning the page of her book to give the impression that she was reading normally. *Supposing the car had broken down and they couldn't come? Or they were delayed for so long that by the time Mam left it would be too late to reach town and meet Gerry?*

Emer closed the book suddenly, unable to keep up the pretence of reading. If the Herlihys didn't come soon, she would have to make up some kind of story. Either way, she *had* to meet Gerry on the dockside.

'Everything all right?' asked Mam.

'Yes, fine,' answered Emer, trying to sound casual as she rose from the table. She would give it five more minutes, she decided as she poured herself a glass of water from the tap. She had just begun to drink, thinking about what she might say, when she heard a welcome sound.

'That's me,' said her mother, recognising the toot on the horn that Mr Herlihy always gave as he pulled up outside the house. 'I'll see you later, Emer. Be good.'

'I will.'

Emer felt a tiny stab of guilt, knowing that if she ended up getting arrested tonight, it would be Mam who would have to sort things out. On impulse she reached out and squeezed her mother's arm. 'Enjoy yourself,' she said, kissing Mam on the cheek.

Her mother looked slightly surprised but smiled at her. 'Thanks, love.'

Emer watched her go, then waited until she heard the Ford driving off down the road. Moving swiftly, she made for the hall, stepped out into the street and slammed the front door shut. She ran towards Jack's house and saw him waiting at the doorway.

'We're behind schedule,' he said.

'Mam was running late. But we can make it in time.'

'OK.'

Emer looked at him squarely. 'You're still on to do this?'

'Of course.'

'Just checking,' she said with a grin. 'All right then. Let's get to town!'

* * *

Gerry stood anxiously on the dockside, upriver of where the Liverpool ferry was berthed. There was constant traffic up and down the quays as horse-drawn cabs, motor cars, vans and foot passengers moved along the busy docks.

He feared that he might look conspicuous as he waited for Emer and Jack, standing against a warehouse wall, his suitcase at his feet. But before he could worry further, he saw them approaching, and he waved with relief.

'Gerry, sorry we're a bit late,' said Emer. 'I thought Mam would never go to bridge.'

'It's sound, you're here now.'

'You got out all right yourself?' asked Jack.

Gerry nodded. 'Yeah, me uncle went straight from work to the pub.'

Emer looked at him sympathetically. 'How do you feel?'

'Nervous … excited … A whole pile of things.'

'You have the police letter?' asked Jack.

Gerry patted his jacket pocket. 'Right here.'

'And you know the drill? Only produce it if you're stopped.'

'Yeah. But before we do all that, I want to tell yis something.' Gerry hesitated, trying to find the right words. 'You were a good school pal, Jack, and now … now you're being a true pal again. Thanks for everything.'

To his surprise, Jack looked moved. 'You're … you're

welcome, Gerry. I really hope it works out for you.'

Gerry nodded in acknowledgement, then he turned to Emer. 'And you've been brilliant, Emer. I don't know what I'd have done without you.'

She shrugged modestly. 'You were great when I was in trouble – one good turn deserves another.'

'It's much more than one good turn.'

'Well, while I'm being brilliant then,' she said with a smile, 'let me give you this.'

Emer handed him an envelope, and Gerry took it uncertainly. 'What is it?'

'It's a letter and … and a few bob that Jack and I scraped together.'

Gerry started to protest, but Emer cut him off. 'Just take it, Gerry. Please. We'll feel much better if we know you're all right.'

'But–'

'No buts. The more money you have, the more it'll give you a start in Liverpool. We want to give it as friends. Take it as a friend.'

Gerry tried to reply but found he had a lump in his throat. Eventually he swallowed hard and gathered himself. 'I'll never forget this. I'll … I'll never forget either of you.'

'We won't forget you either,' said Jack.

'And what's in the letter?'

Emer looked slightly uncomfortable. 'Just a few things I wanted to say. Promise you won't open it till you're safely on the boat. OK?'

'OK.'

'We should make a move,' suggested Jack.

'God, I hope this works,' said Gerry.

Jack nodded grimly. 'We're all sunk if it doesn't.'

'Then let's think positively,' said Emer. 'And … we should probably say our goodbyes now.'

Jack shook his friend's hand warmly and wished him luck. Gerry turned and offered Emer his hand too. She shook it firmly and wished him well, then she suddenly reached out and hugged him. Gerry was deeply moved, but he couldn't afford to draw attention to himself by arriving at the ferry teary-eyed. Instead he held Emer tightly for a moment, then stepped back.

'Right,' he said softly. 'Let's do it.'

* * *

The uniformed policeman stood on the busy quayside, scanning the crowd. A typical DMP officer, he was over six feet tall, and even from a distance, Emer could see him towering above the people congregating near the ramp leading onto the ferry.

She felt her mouth go dry as she walked alongside Jack, and she tried hard to maintain a casual demeanour. They were several paces behind Gerry. It had been agreed that he should act as though he were travelling alone and not acknowledge their presence.

The nearer they got to the ship, the more horse-drawn cabs, motor cars and foot passengers milled about, and Emer hoped that the busyness of the scene would work in Gerry's favour. Jack reckoned there would be plain-clothes police officers in addition to the uniformed constables, but in the aftermath of the Rising they would be watching for known republicans, and Emer told herself that they wouldn't be scrutinising youngsters.

The ordinary police, however, would observe everyone. Gerry had grown in recent months and was now tall for his age, and Emer prayed that that would be enough to get him past the policeman without drawing attention.

Jack and Emer continued towards the ship, matching Gerry's pace. They had decided that Gerry should walk confidently, but not so quickly as to attract notice. Now, as they drew nearer to the DMP officer, Emer felt her heart pounding. She tried to follow the advice that Jack had given Gerry: *Stay calm, don't catch the policeman's eye, but don't look furtive either.*

Emer realised that it was one thing to talk about appearing cool, another thing to act that way under pressure. Still, Gerry's stride hadn't become hesitant. She held her breath as the moment of truth arrived. Gerry glanced casually up at the deck of the ship as he drew level with the DMP officer, and Emer felt like cheering his cool demeanour. *He was going to make it!*

Emer turned to Jack and smiled. Then she heard the policeman calling out: 'Just a second, sonny.'

She saw Gerry stop, and she dropped to one knee and pretended to tie her shoelace. Jack hovered nearby but out of the constable's line of sight.

'Where are you off to?' asked the policeman.

'Liverpool, sir,' said Gerry.

'Who are you going with?'

'Just meself. But it's OK, I have a ticket bought and all.'

'Really? How old are you?'

'I'll be fourteen on me next birthday. Here's the ticket.'

Emer thought Gerry was handling himself well as she continued to fuss with her lace. She hoped the constable would be satisfied with Gerry's ticket. There was a moment's pause as he examined it.

'That seems to be in order. But why is there nobody with you?'

'Me mother has to mind me sick sister. And me da was wounded at the Somme. I'm going to see him in a hospital in England. It's all in this letter, sir. Here you are,' said Gerry, handing it over.

Emer watched as the constable read the letter, her stomach knotted with fear. Jack had claimed that any uniformed officers on the docks would most likely be from B Division of the DMP – and therefore they wouldn't serve under Inspector Rooney of A Division, whose signature he had forged. *But supposing this constable had served under Rooney in the past and knew his signature?* It seemed unlikely, but he was taking an age to consider the letter.

'This is unusual,' he said finally.

'That's why me ma went to the police station to get the letter.'

'She went to all that trouble, but she couldn't get someone to travel with you? An aunt, an uncle?'

'She couldn't get anyone, sir.'

'You've a Dublin accent. You must have relations here.'

Emer didn't like the way this was going. The constable hadn't voiced suspicion about the letter itself, but he seemed unconvinced by the rest of Gerry's story. She glanced over at Jack, wondering what to do. He gave a quick shake of the head and Emer waited, hoping

Gerry could persuade the policeman.

'I do have an aunt and an uncle. But he's out of work, and they couldn't shell out for a boat ticket. I mean, I'm well able to travel meself.'

'Maybe you are. Then again, maybe not. If your father's a soldier, he's earning proper wages. Why couldn't your mother buy a ticket for your uncle?'

'We … we need the money,' said Gerry. 'Me da's badly injured. He won't be earning as a soldier any more.'

'He'll get disability pay. Surely your mother knows that.'

Emer was afraid that Gerry wouldn't be able to lie his way out of trouble for much longer. She looked to Jack, and this time he nodded.

Before Gerry had the chance to answer the constable, Jack cried out, 'He has a knife!'

Emer rose from her knees and grabbed the constable's sleeve. 'Oh my God!' she said, pointing towards the thick of the crowd. 'That man's pulled a knife!'

The constable looked around in confusion.

'He'll stab someone!' cried Emer.

The policeman looked to see who Emer was pointing at, and Gerry quickly put out his hand. 'Can I have me letter back?'

The policeman hesitated for what could only have

been a split second, but it seemed an eternity to Emer. Then he swiftly thrust the letter into Gerry's hand. 'Where's the man?' he snapped at Emer.

'He's run into the crowd, sir!' said Jack. 'Over there!'

'He's making for the laneway!' cried Emer.

She watched as the constable barged through the thickest part of the crowd, heading towards a nearby lane, then she and Jack turned and walked quickly in the opposite direction. They made for the nearest road junction, and just as they reached the corner and safety, Emer looked back. Passengers were streaming up the gangplank onto the ferry. Gerry, to her huge relief, was nowhere to be seen.

CHAPTER ELEVEN

The last golden beams of light were dimming and the summer dusk was taking hold. A crescent moon was rising in the sky as Gerry stood on the upper deck of the ferry. He heard the throbbing of the engines increase, then the mooring ropes were thrown aboard and the ship moved away from the quayside.

Gerry exhaled slowly, finally allowing himself to relax as the boat pulled out into the waters of the River Liffey. Up to this point he had feared a tap on the shoulder, some last-minute hitch that would undo his getaway. But now the ferry was travelling down the river towards Dublin Bay and the open sea.

Thanks to Emer and Jack, he had escaped. His mind was racing with conflicting thoughts. He loved the idea of having out-smarted Thomas Byrne, and he savoured the image of the blackmailer waiting impatiently at lunchtime today, wondering why Gerry hadn't shown up. He was pleased also to get away from Uncle Pat and his drink-fuelled mood swings. At the same time, Gerry resented having to leave Ireland to make a new life in a place where he knew nobody.

The rebels had read out a Proclamation on the first day of the Rising, stating that in their vision of Ireland all the children of the nation would be cherished equally. But Gerry knew instinctively that when it came to people like him, that wouldn't happen. Or maybe one day it would, but for now the poor would still be treated badly, like they always had been. So he would make his own way, in Liverpool or wherever else he might end up.

Other passengers were looking back upriver, seeking a final view of the city as the boat made its way through the port. Gerry resisted the temptation to look back. Dublin had rarely given him a break, and he wouldn't get sentimental about the city now. Instead he stared straight ahead, looking to sea as the ship began to pick up speed.

✳ ✳ ✳

Emer sat beside Jack on the upper deck of the tram. She gazed out the window as they trundled northwards towards home, her mood reflective. She and Jack had hurried away from the docks, then on reaching the city centre, they had laughed and shaken hands, thrilled that their diversion had worked.

Emer reckoned that Gerry's ship would be on its way by now, and she wondered what lay in store for him in England. She hoped that it would all work out and sensed that whatever came his way, Gerry would make the best of it and do well. She was pleased, too, that she and Jack had managed to stay close friends despite their families being on opposite sides during the death and destruction of the Rising, and that they had joined forces once more in helping Gerry.

Thinking of her family, she wished Dad wasn't still a prisoner in the camp at Frongoch. But at least he was alive and recovering from his wounds, and she and Mam were running their two shops profitably. Eventually Dad would be with them again.

'Penny for your thoughts,' said Jack.

Emer grinned sheepishly, aware that she had been miles away. 'Just thinking that … well, things will probably all come good in the end.'

'What things?'

'Things for Gerry … for me and you … for my dad. Even for Dublin itself.'

'Yeah?'

'It'll be rebuilt eventually, and …'

'And what?' prompted Jack.

'And I'm glad we saw all that happened. We've lived

through history in the making, Jack. We even played a small part in it.'

Jack nodded. 'I suppose we did, at that. But I think I've had enough of history for now.'

'Yeah,' said Emer thoughtfully. 'Maybe we should leave the past and move on.' Then she smiled at her friend, sat back in her seat and let the tram carry them home.

* * *

Gerry stood on the ship's deck. Ahead of him, where the Liffey met the bay, he could see the Poolbeg Light-house illuminating the dusk. Gerry held Emer's letter in his hand, and although the sky was darkening, there was still enough light to read the single sheet of paper. Emer had enclosed five shillings that she and Jack had managed to raise, and Gerry gratefully slipped the money into his pocket. Then he started to read her message.

Dear Gerry,

If you're reading this on the ship then you'll have escaped, so congratulations!

But I'm really, really sorry you have to run away from home, it's all wrong, and I wish I could have done more to help you.

I want to live in a better Ireland, where brave boys like you don't have to leave. That's the Ireland my dad fought for, and that's the Ireland I'll try to bring about.

Do well in England, Gerry, and look after yourself. But please come back some day. And don't forget me and Jack. I'll never, ever forget you.

Your friend,

Emer Davey

Gerry read the letter through, and his eyes welled up. This time he didn't have to hide his feelings, and he allowed a tear to roll down his cheek. Maybe there was hope for Ireland, he thought, if people like Emer became the ones in charge.

He read the letter again, then slipped it into his pocket. He dried his eyes, his spirits buoyed by its message. Perhaps he had been wrong to turn his back deliberately on Dublin. Everyone wasn't like his uncle, or Thomas Byrne; there were good people there too, like Mr Mac and Jack and Emer. Maybe someday he would come back … Who could tell? Now, though, it was time for a final farewell.

He turned around, leaned over the rail of the boat and gazed back upriver. Gaslights along the docks reflected on the water, and in the distance he could see the brighter lights of the city centre. He watched for a long time as Dublin gradually fell away behind him. Then he turned away and looked out to sea, ready now to face the future.

EPILOGUE

MR MADIGAN never discovered Jack's deception with the forged letter. He continued serving as a policeman after the DMP was absorbed into An Garda Síochána, the police force of the new Irish Free State. The Madigans lived on Ellesmere Avenue for many years, but Jack moved to London, where he had a long and successful career with the BBC in the new medium of radio.

Ben followed his father into the family's electrical business, and Gladys went on to become vice-principal of her old school. Joan worked in an office before meeting an American naval officer. She married him and raised a family in San Diego, in a house she nostalgically named 'Tolka Fields'.

Mrs Davey and Emer kept the family business going during Mr Davey's imprisonment; it would eventually expand to five shops. Emer studied commerce and helped to run, and eventually manage, the family's grocery stores. She married a classmate of Ben's, exchanged Christmas cards every year with Jack, and remained friends with Gladys and Ben for the rest of her life.

Uncle Pat took Gerry at his word and didn't come looking for him. They never met again. Gerry got a job in Liverpool, in the stables of a dealer who provided horses to the British Army. He remained in England until the end of the First World War, then emigrated to New Zealand, where he made a new life as a horse breeder. He married, had a family, and never returned to Ireland. But he wrote regularly to Emer and Jack, and every year on September 1st – the anniversary of his escape – he raised a celebratory glass of Irish whiskey and toasted the two best friends he had ever known.

HISTORICAL NOTE

ROGER CASEMENT was the last of the sixteen rebel leaders to be executed in the aftermath of the Easter Rising. The rebels imprisoned by the British authorities in Frongoch Camp in Wales began to be released in batches, and by December 1916 the last prisoners were freed and returned to Ireland. A little over five years later, following the bloody War of Independence, the Irish Free State came into being in January 1922.

The First World War ended in November 1918, by which time an estimated sixteen million people had been killed. Over 200,000 Irishmen are thought to have fought in the British Army, of whom more than 30,000 were killed.

Sackville Street (now O'Connell Street) was rebuilt after the Rising, but was damaged further during the Irish Civil War. It was finally restored after the Civil War ended in 1923.

One Good Turn is a work of fiction, and the families of Emer, Jack, Gerry and their friends are figments of my imagination. The historical events referred to are real, however, and the looting during the Rising, the fad for ukulele music, the Battle of the Somme and the Armenian massacre were all actual events.

The River Tolka was a popular spot for swimming, but Gerry's cottage is fictitious – its location would now be part of the Tolka Valley Park. The cattle market on Prussia Street, where Emer and Gerry met, was built upon in the 1970s, but Ellesmere Avenue is a real place and has changed little in the years since 1916.

Brian Gallagher,
Dublin 2016

Other Books by
Brian Gallagher

The prequel to *One Good Turn*

Friend or Foe

It's time to choose:
friends, family or loyalty to the cause

When Emer Davey saves her neighbour Jack Madigan
from drowning, it seems that they'll be friends forever.
But eight months later, they find themselves on opposite sides in a life-or-death struggle, as Dublin is torn
apart by the 1916 Easter Rising – and the violence
hits closer to home than either could have imagined.

Across the Divide

What happens when your best friend ought to be your enemy?

Liam's father is a proud trade-union member, while Nora's is a prosperous wine importer. When Jim Larkin takes on the employers in the 1913 Dublin Lockout, the friends find that their loyalties are put to the test.

Taking Sides

A boy. A girl. A nation torn apart.

On a scholarship to Eccles Street School, Annie makes friends with wealthy Susie and her brother Peter. But civil war is brewing, and when hotheaded Peter gets involved with the rebels, it has grave repercussions for all of them.

Secrets and Shadows

Can you trust anyone in a time of war?

In the summer of 1941, friends Grace and Barry begin to suspect their sports coach of spying for the Nazis. They are determined to find proof, but what starts as an exciting challenge becomes increasingly risky.

Stormclouds

Can old differences ever be overcome?

Twins Emma and Dylan move from America to Belfast in the late 1960s, where they make friends from both loyalist and nationalist backgrounds. When political tensions boil over into violence, it is not just their friendships that are threatened – but their lives too.

WORLD BOOK DAY *fest*

Want to **READ** more?

YOUR LOCAL BOOKSHOP

- Get some great recommendations for what to read next
- Meet your favourite authors & illustrators at brilliant events
- Discover books you never even knew existed!

  www.booksellers.org.uk/bookshopsearch

YOUR LOCAL LIBRARY

You can browse and borrow from a HUGE selection of books and get recommendations of what to read next from expert librarians—all for **FREE**! You can also discover libraries' wonderful childr and family reading activit

  www.findalibrary.co.uk

GET ONLINE

VISIT **WORLDBOOKDAY.COM** TO DISCOVER A WHOLE NEW WORLD OF BOOKS

- Downloads and activities for top books and authors
- Cool games, trailers and videos
- Author events in your area
- News, competitions and new books—all in a FREE monthly email

AND MORE!